EMEKA'S GIFT

An African Counting Story

EMEKA'S GIFT

An African Counting Story

IFEOMA ONYEFULU

PUFFIN BOOKS

To my parents Emmanuel and Emily, and to my son, Emeka,
for being a wonderful traveling companion.

PUFFIN BOOKS
Published by the Penguin Group
Penguin Putnam Inc., 375 Hudson Street, New York, New York 10014, U.S.A.
Penguin Books Ltd, 27 Wrights Lane, London W8 5TZ, England
Penguin Books Australia Ltd, Ringwood, Victoria, Australia
Penguin Books Canada Ltd, 10 Alcorn Avenue, Toronto, Ontario, Canada M4V 3B2
Penguin Books (N.Z.) Ltd, 182-190 Wairau Road, Auckland 10, New Zealand

Penguin Books Ltd, Registered Offices: Harmondsworth, Middlesex, England

First published in the United States of America by Cobblehill Books, an affiliate of Dutton Children's Books,
a division of Penguin Books USA Inc., 1995
Originally published in Great Britain by Frances Lincoln Limited, London, 1995
Published by Puffin Books, a member of Penguin Putnam Books for Young Readers, 1999

3 5 7 9 10 8 6 4 2

Emeka's Gift copyright © Frances Lincoln Limited, 1995
Text and photographs copyright © Ifeoma Onyefulu, 1995
All rights reserved

THE LIBRARY OF CONGRESS HAS CATALOGED THE COBBLEHILL EDITION AS FOLLOWS:
Onyefulu, Ifeoma.
Emeka's gift: an African counting story / Ifeoma Onyefulu.
p. cm.
ISBN 0-525-65205-1
1. Africa—Social life and customs—Juvenile literature. 2. Counting—Juvenile literature.
I: Title: DT3.059 1995 960—dc20 94-30700 CIP AC

Puffin Books ISBN 0-14-056500-0

Printed in the United States of America

A Note from the Author

Emeka, the little boy in this book, lives in a village called Ibaji, in southern Nigeria, and comes from a tribe called Igala. The Igala people, who speak the Kwa language, are traders, farmers, fishermen and healers.

Most of the objects I have photographed are made by hand, with older family members passing on their skills to the younger ones. Some things are used every day: brooms to clear the compounds, hats for working out in the hot sun, pestles and mortars for pounding up food - a sound heard before mealtimes even in the cities. Other things are brought out on special occasions, like the musical *ishaka*, and the colourful necklaces women wear for important village events.

In many parts of Africa, grandmothers play a vital family role helping to bring up the children. When children visit their grandparents, they are often given a present, perhaps of homegrown fruit and vegetables - and sometimes the children give a present in return. As Emeka daydreams of all the things he could take his grandmother, he shows just how much he loves her.

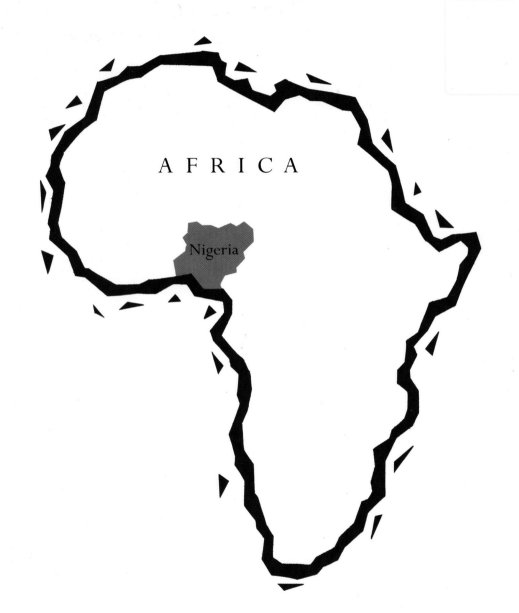

1

One boy who was not too small, but not too big either, set off to visit his grandmother in the next village. His name was Emeka.

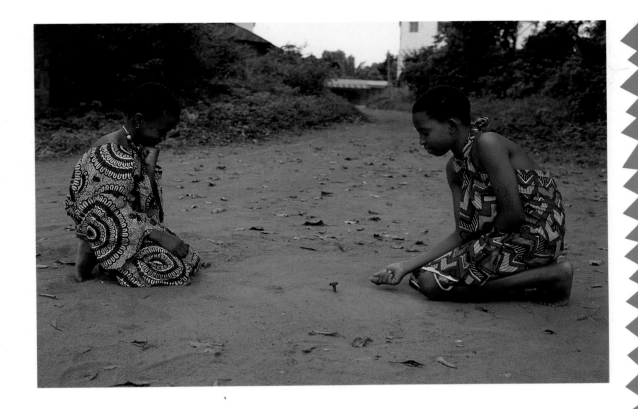

Okoso

Children play this game with spinning tops, empty snail shells - or anything that spins. These girls are playing with a used pen top. The player whose okoso spins the longest is the winner.

2

Two of Emeka's friends, Bola and Ada, were kneeling on the path playing *okoso*, his favourite game.

Emeka smiled as he passed them, but he didn't stop because he was thinking, "What can I take Granny as a present?"

3

Three women on their way to market turned to say hello to Emeka. "There must be lots of things in the market that Granny would like," he thought, walking that way too.

Markets

Markets are important meeting-places for people from villages all around. The local chief is always there to act as chief official. As well as buying food, clothes and household things, you can get your hair plaited and your bicycle repaired at the local market.

4

Four new brooms were propped up against a wall.

"Wouldn't it be nice if Granny had one of those," said Emeka, "for sweeping away the leaves that fall down from the orange and mango trees."

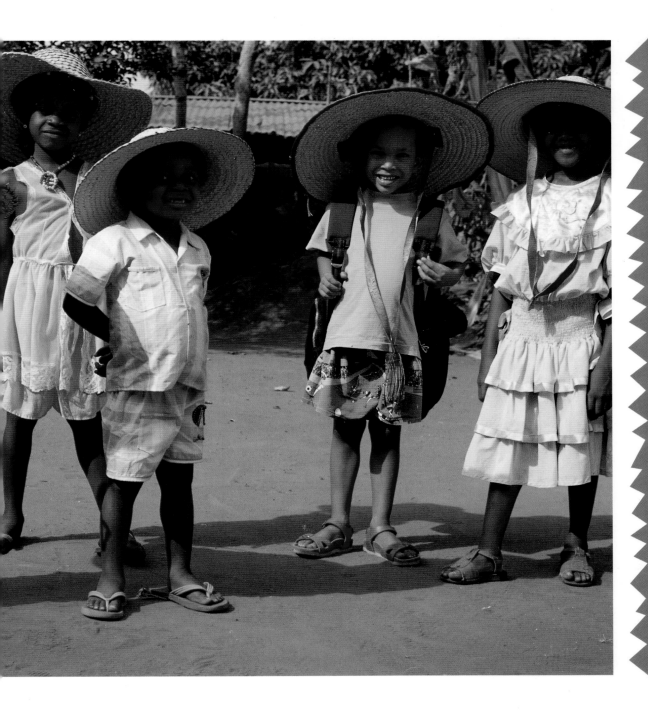

5

Five children dressed up in big grown-up hats smiled and waved at Emeka.

"What lovely hats!" he said. "Granny might like one of those to keep out the sun when she goes to the farm or to market."

6

Six beautiful beaded necklaces were set out on display.

"My sister Oge wears beads like those," said Emeka. "Granny might say, 'Child, I am far too old for necklaces!' but I think she would look just as lovely as Oge."

Necklaces

Young women and children wear them all the time, old women just for special occasions. Some necklaces are made from the dried seeds of the *akodegbe* plant, and some from glass or dyed rubber beads.

7

Seven musical instruments called *ishaka* caught Emeka's eye. Nearby, two girls were trying to play them like grown-up musicians.

Emeka laughed.

"With those ishaka, Granny's dance group would be a big hit when they perform for the village."

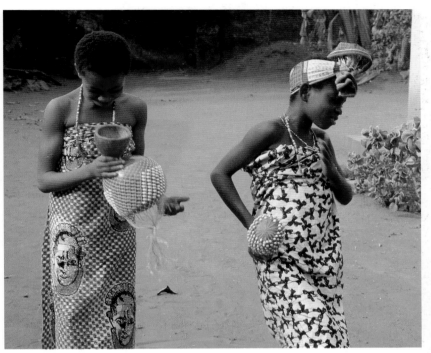

Ishaka

These musical instruments are made from natural or red-dyed gourds hung with dried seeds from the akodegbe plant, or with pieces of cooked, dyed rubber taken from the rubber tree. Shaken from side to side, they make a distinctive soft, rattling sound.

8

Eight water-pots, some tall, some small, stood on sale by the roadside. Emeka looked them up and down.

"With pots like those, Granny could store water for days and days, and give the garden plenty to drink. Then her tomatoes would grow bigger than ever."

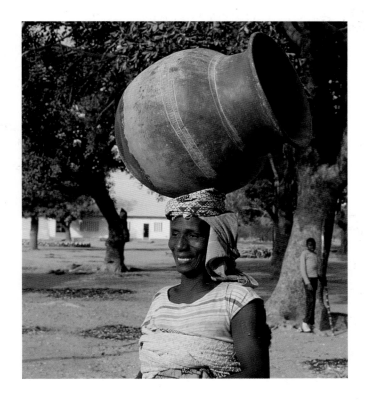

Water

In many African countries, the year is divided into rainy and dry seasons. People store water in earthenware pots, in plastic containers and in huge water tanks to use during the dry season, which lasts for several months.

9

Nine mortars and some pestles were lined up in rows at the end of the market.

"Some of those would be good for Granny's kitchen," thought Emeka. "Then, when I visit her with my cousins, we could help her to pound up yams for supper.

But with no money, I can't give her anything." He walked slowly up to his grandmother's house.

Pestles and mortars

Pestles and mortars are used for grinding up food. The wood-carver makes them from a tree trunk, hollowing out a piece very carefully to make the mortar. The pestle is shaped to make it easy to handle and to grind up different kinds of food.

10

Ten of Emeka's cousins were there, waiting to play with him. Emeka ran to tell his grandmother about all the things he wanted to bring her. But she just gave him a big hug, and said, "Child, you're the best present of all!"

Families

In many parts of Africa, a typical family household includes three generations, and the doors are always open to aunts, uncles and cousins - so there is someone to look after the children when the parents are out.

Other Picture Books
from Puffin